The Chalk Rainbow

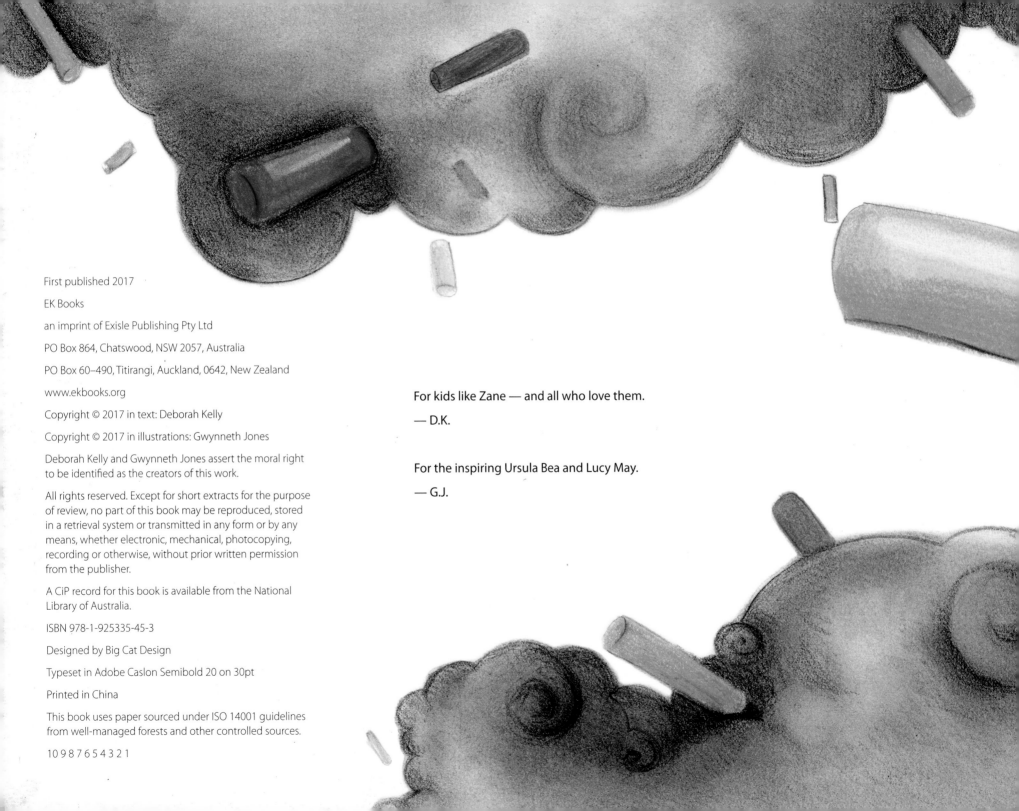

First published 2017

EK Books

an imprint of Exisle Publishing Pty Ltd

PO Box 864, Chatswood, NSW 2057, Australia

PO Box 60–490, Titirangi, Auckland, 0642, New Zealand

www.ekbooks.org

A CiP record for this book is available from the National Library of Australia.

ISBN 978-1-925335-45-3

Designed by Big Cat Design

Typeset in Adobe Caslon Semibold 20 on 30pt

Printed in China

This book uses paper sourced under ISO 14001 guidelines from well-managed forests and other controlled sources.

10 9 8 7 6 5 4 3 2 1

For kids like Zane — and all who love them.

— D.K.

For the inspiring Ursula Bea and Lucy May.

— G.J.

The Chalk Rainbow

Deborah Kelly and **Gwynneth Jones**

My brother Zane is different to other kids.

He's got his own made-up language.

He likes to line things up.

And he *hates* the colour black.

Zane won't eat black food — not even liquorice!

He won't wear black clothes, either.

My brother Zane won't even *walk*
across anything that is black …

Like the pedestrian crossing.

Or the soft fall at the playground.

Or our driveway.

Dad gets mad at Zane.

Mama tries hard to explain things to him, but Zane just scrunches himself into a ball …

and *screams!*

So I start a chalk rainbow, at the top of
our front steps, to cheer him up.

People walking past stop and smile.

They talk to me and Zane.

We just **keep on colouring.**

Zane and I pretend the driveway is the water, and our rainbow is a bridge.

We run back and forth across our rainbow bridge.

Zane wants to make another rainbow
bridge — but there's no more chalk!

Then I look at our chalky fingers
and I have an idea.

I show Zane a *different* way
to make a rainbow bridge.

Zane holds my hand very, very tightly.

Up, up and over we go ... down to the other side.

We make rainbow bridge ... after rainbow bridge ...
after rainbow bridge ... **until there are rainbow bridges all
over our driveway ...** and our backyard!

Our parents want to make a rainbow bridge, too.
So Zane and I show them how.

Soon there are rainbows *everywhere!*

Together,

we make rainbow bridges

right along the footpath …

over the pedestrian crossing …

and across the soft fall
at the playground …

All the way …

... home.

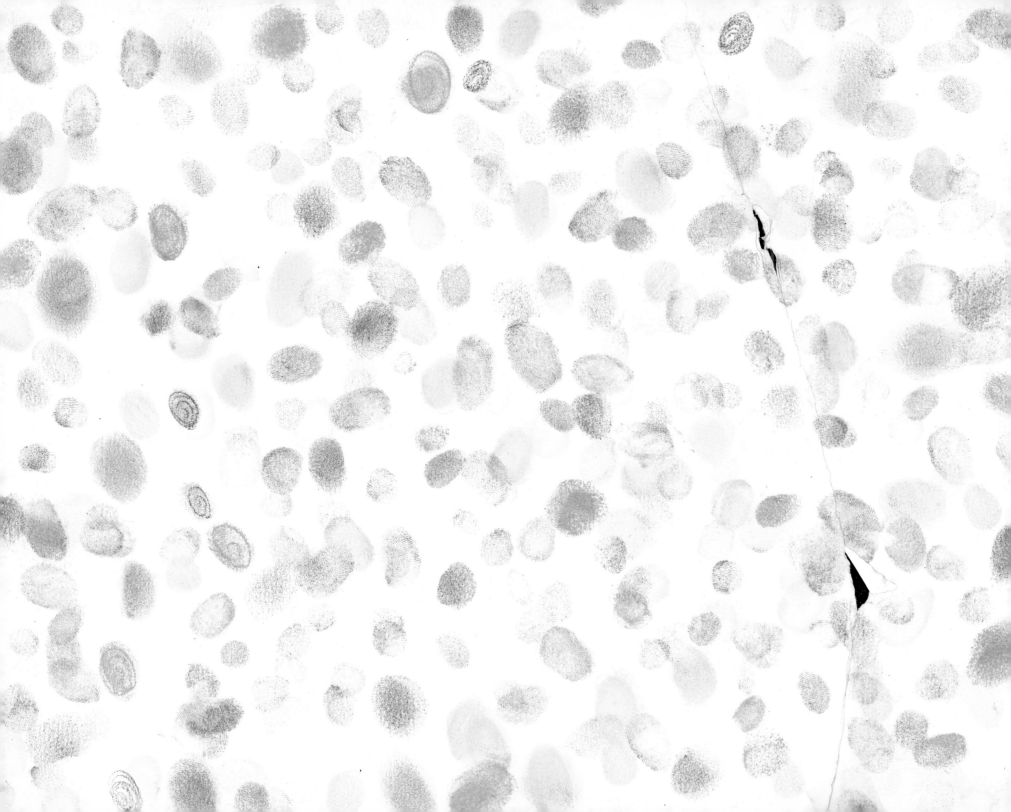